MARCUS SEDGWICK
CUDWEED'S BIRTHDAY

Illustrated by Pete Williamson

Orion
Children's Books

First published in Great Britain in 2011
by Orion Children's Books
a division of the Orion Publishing Group Ltd
Orion House
5 Upper Saint Martin's Lane
London WC2H 9EA
An Hachette UK Company

1 3 5 7 9 10 8 6 4 2

A catalogue record for this book is available from the British Library.

ISBN 978 1 4440 0319 2

Printed in China

www.orionbooks.co.uk
www.ravenmysteries.co.uk

To everyone who has a birthday

CONTENTS

CHAPTER 1   9

CHAPTER 2   25

CHAPTER 3   39

CHAPTER 4   57

CHAPTER 5   71

CHAPTER 1

This is Cudweed.

If you think *he* looks funny,
you should see his mum

and his dad.

He has a big sister too, and she looks like this, almost normal.

Almost.

If you think they all look a bit odd,
you'd be right, but then, this is where
they live.

And you couldn't live in a crazy castle like that and be normal, could you?

It's the sort of place where **odd** and **strange** things happen. A lot. And this is the story of the **odd** and **strange** things that happened on Cudweed's tenth birthday…

Cudweed felt excited.
It was his tenth birthday, and a tenth
birthday is a good reason to
be excited.

But he was worried too. He was
worried for lots of reasons; the main
reason was that he worries an awful
lot of the time anyway, but he was
also worrying just then about
his birthday.

Supposing it wasn't as exciting as it
should be?
Supposing they had a birthday party
and there were not enough crisps?
Or none at all?

And worst of all, supposing that
he didn't get what he wanted for
his birthday?!

The result of feeling excited and worried was that Cudweed looked like this.

His big sister, Solstice (you say it like this: "Sol-stiss"), walked past him in a corridor on the day before his birthday, and found him staring into space.

He looked as though he had turned
into a stone statue, but in fact,
he was thinking.

Now thinking is one of the things
that Cudweed finds difficult. He's not
very good at it, and so usually he tries
not to do it at all.

'Are you quite all right, Cudweed?' asked Solstice. There was a large, old, cross-looking raven sitting on her shoulder.
Cudweed didn't answer.
Solstice nodded.

'He's thinking,' she whispered to the raven.

'Ark,' said the raven, as quietly as he could.

'Shh!' said Solstice, holding the bird's beak shut. 'It's not a good idea to wake him when he's thinking. It could do serious damage.'
She thought for a moment, then shrugged.
'Oh well,' she said, and tugged her brother hard on the shoulder.
'Hey! Cudweed! What's going on?'

Cudweed jumped, as if a goat had bitten his bottom.
He spun around, looking terrified, but calmed down when he saw Solstice.

'Well,' he said, 'I've been thinking…'

'Yes,' said Solstice. 'We could tell.'

'I've been thinking, and I think I have thought of something terrible.'

'Go on,' said Solstice, tickling the raven under his chin.

'Well,' said Cudweed. 'I've been worrying about what will happen if I don't get what I want for my birthday tomorrow.'

'Really?'

'Yes. But the thing is, I have just realised that I do not know what I want for my birthday. And if I do not know what I want, how will I know if I don't get it?'

'That is a very big thing to worry about,' Solstice said.

'But don't worry, Cudweed, because I think I know just what you want for your birthday.'

'You do?' asked Cudweed.

'I do! Follow me!'

Solstice led the way down the corridor, and Cudweed ran after her, feeling a little less worried, and a little bit more excited.

CHAPTER 2

Solstice took Cudweed along the corridor, down a passage, and up a very long and creaky staircase.

'Where are we going?'
Cudweed asked.

'Here,' said Solstice, and she stopped
in front of a door.

'I know where we are,' Cudweed said slowly. He squinted at the door.

'I hope so,' said Solstice.
'It's your bedroom.'

'I thought so,' said Cudweed quickly.
Then he added, 'But why are we here?'

'I want to show you something.'
Solstice opened the door and they
went into Cudweed's bedroom.

It is a large room, and at one end
there is a smaller room, hidden
behind a curtain.

On the curtain there is a sign.
The sign says

Solstice ignored it, and pulled back
the curtain.

'Hey!' cried Cudweed, but Solstice
ignored him too.

'This,' she said, 'is what you would like for your birthday, isn't it?'

On the floor were lots of large boxes. They were old cardboard boxes, which Cudweed had spent a long time cutting into pieces, and then sticking back together, so that they made a tiny little town.

He had made a sign too, which said

Cudweed's Zoo

and the sign hung above the biggest box. Cudweed looked confused.

'But,' he said, 'I already have it.'

'It's there.'

'Yes, I know that,' said Solstice.
'I don't mean your zoo. What I mean
is, what you want for your birthday,
is something that would go in a zoo.'

Cudweed looked more confused.
'A visitor?' he asked.

'No!' said Solstice. 'An animal!'
'What you want,' said Solstice, 'is a
real animal! Look what you've got in
your zoo.'
She waved her hand at the boxes.

It's true, thought Cudweed.
The animals in his zoo were made of
paper, or card, or wood, or plastic,
or leaves, or cotton wool, or string,
or fluff.

'So what you mean,' he said very, very slowly, 'is that I should have an animal of my own.'

Solstice nodded.

'A real one.'

'Yes,' said Solstice.

'One that I could keep in the castle. Here. In my own room.'

'Yes' said Solstice.

Cudweed smiled. For a moment, he didn't look worried. Not one little bit. 'You mean . . . a pet?'

'Yes,' said Solstice.

Cudweed smiled some more, then suddenly the smile disappeared from his face.

'What is it?' asked Solstice.

'But I don't know what pet I want.'
His bottom lip trembled and he
looked as if he was going to cry.

'But! Brother! Don't worry! I know
where we can go to get good ideas
about pets!'

'You do?' asked Cudweed, looking happier again.
'I do!' cried Solstice. 'Follow me! Again!'

CHAPTER 3

Soon they were standing in front of a shop window.

They had walked out of the castle,
down the long twisty drive, and
into town.
The raven had flown off somewhere.

Solstice said she thought he was
sulking, but for now, they had other
things to think about.

The pet shop was called Catchem's.

Cudweed pushed his nose against the window, leaving a mark on the glass.

He stared for a long time, blinking and thinking.

'Well, Cudweed,' said Solstice. 'Do you see anything you like?'

Cudweed nodded.
'It would be a good idea,' he said,
'to go inside.'

They went inside, and Cudweed
looked at the cages and tanks and
pens and hutches, seeing what was in
each and every one.

There were hamsters, and chicks, and mice, and fish, and more fish, and rabbits, and big fluffy things that weren't rabbits, but that Cudweed didn't know the name of, and lots and lots of other things too.

Mr Catchem, the man who owned the shop came over to them.

'May I help you?' he asked.

'Possibly,' said Solstice. 'We're looking for ideas. It's Cudweed's birthday tomorrow.'

'I see,' said Mr Catchem.
'Well, be sure to come back when you've decided. We have all your pet needs here!'

Solstice and Cudweed nodded and smiled and left the shop.

'Well?' asked Solstice.

'Well,' said Cudweed. 'There are some very nice animals in that shop. Very nice. But somehow . . . '

'Somehow, what?' asked Solstice. Cudweed was about to answer when they heard a

loud

noise.

From around the corner came a marching, banging, tooting, shouting, stamping, trumpeting parade.

'The circus has come to town!'
cried Solstice.
She was right!
Clowns and acrobats and jugglers, and
lorries and caravans and clown-cars,
and a lot of animals filled the street.

There were tigers, and lions, and
elephants, and monkeys, and horses,
and snakes, and . . .

Suddenly Cudweed shouted.

Solstice nearly jumped out of her skin. 'What is it?' she cried.

'That!' shouted Cudweed. 'Those! There! That one! Them!

I know what kind of pet I want now.'
He flapped his hands.

'I want one of them!'

Solstice looked very serious.
'Oh,' she said. 'You know, I don't think Mother and Father are going to like this.'

They did not.
They did not like it one bit.
Cudweed stood in front of them at
supper time, blinking, and telling
them why it would be a really good
idea if he had a python for a pet.

But Cudweed's mum and dad were
not at all impressed, and their final
word on the subject was 'No.'
Cudweed's mother shook her head.

'It simply can't be done.'

Cudweed's bottom lip began to wobble . . .

His father whispered something to his mother, and his mother whispered back. 'Listen,' she said to Cudweed. 'To cheer you up, why don't we give you a present now?

It's not your birthday till the morning,
but you may as well have this one
tonight. Would you like that?'

Cudweed nodded, and took a small
brown envelope from his mother.

He looked puzzled.

'Open it!' whispered Solstice, and when he did, Cudweed's tears dried up.

It was two tickets for the circus on Cudweed's birthday.
And what a day that turned out to be!

CHAPTER 4

Cudweed woke up early.
It was his birthday after all.
After he'd woken up, he spent a long
time asking Solstice to get up too,
and then opened some presents from
his family.

The presents weren't very exciting.
There were some socks and a boring
jumper, but Cudweed didn't seem
to mind.

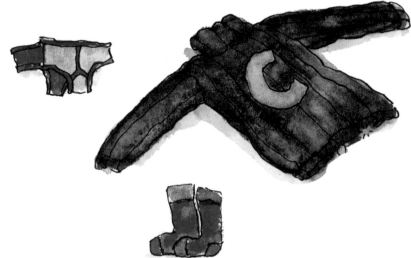

For one thing, he and his big sister were off to the circus that morning, and for another, as he said to Solstice on the way down the drive, 'I expect they're saving my big present for tea-time.'

'Your big present?' asked Solstice.

'Yes. You know. A gorilla.
Or a giant lizard.'

Solstice couldn't think what to say to that.

Because they had got up so early, they were very early arriving at the circus. In fact, they had over an hour to wait before the gates opened, and another hour to wait before the show started.

It was during that time that the Bad Thing happened.

Cudweed was bored.
Solstice was bored.

They'd spent a long time looking
around the circus, and all the tents,
and all the caravans, but now, they
were bored.

'Shall we get something to eat?'
Cudweed said.

'You can,' said Solstice.
'I'm not hungry.'

So Cudweed went off by himself and
came back holding a hot-dog in one
hand, and a stick of candy-floss in
the other.

There was no one about.
He blinked.
He took a bite of hot-dog, and a nibble
of candy-floss.
He looked around.
Still no one in sight.
And then he went and had a chat to
the animals.
He stopped by the elephant.

It was in a very large cage, but it was a very large elephant, and it looked squashed and squished inside the cage. Cudweed looked deep into its eyes.

He thought it was sad.

I expect, he thought, it's not very
happy being stuck inside that cage.
I expect it would like to get out.
For a bit. And stretch its legs.
Cudweed shoved the candy-floss
up to the bars of the cage, and the
elephant happily ate the lot.
It seemed to like it, but it still
seemed unhappy.

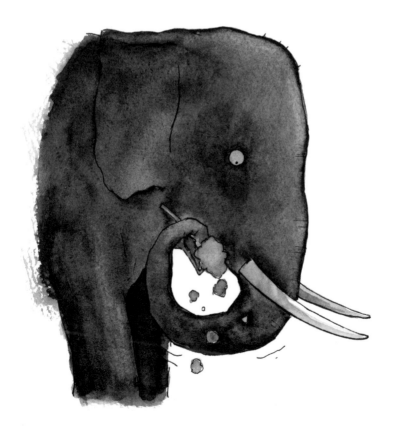

That's when Cudweed saw the bolt on the cage, and it was not long after that that he opened the door, and it was not long after that that there was a giant elephant running around the circus.

The elephant ran into tents and caravans and other cages and before long the whole circus was a very noisy and messy mess.

Cudweed and Solstice ran all the way home.

'Oh goodness!' their mother said. 'I'm so glad you're all right. Have you heard? There's an elephant running wild at the circus! Did you see it?'

Solstice looked at Cudweed.
'Did you see it?' she asked.

Cudweed shook his head.

'No,' he said, in a quiet voice.
'I don't know anything about it at
all and I wasn't there when nothing
happened.'

Solstice and Cudweed's mother
looked at him.
For a long time.
'Really?' said Solstice.

CHAPTER 5

It wasn't just the elephant that was
a problem.

As it had crashed and bashed around
the cages at the circus, it had broken
some of them.

So now there were also tigers, bears,
horses and other animals all bashing
around the place too.

'You have to do something,' Solstice said to Cudweed.

'Why?' asked Cudweed.

'Because this is your fault!' cried Solstice. 'I know it is. You can say what you like, but I know this had something to do with you. Didn't it?'

She stared at Cudweed.
His bottom lip wobbled…
'Yes,' he said. 'It did.'

'Well, then. It's up to you to sort it out.'

'Is it?' asked Cudweed,
looking scared.

'Yes,' said Solstice. 'It is. But I'll help.'

By the time they got back to town,
most of the animals had been caught
by the people who worked at the
circus, but there were still one or two
little things hopping about, and a
few monkeys.

And one very large
and very cross elephant.

'What are we going to do?'
Solstice asked.

Cudweed looked worried.
The elephant was still running
around, as if it had gone slightly mad.
People were trying to get it back into
its cage, but with no luck.

Suddenly Cudweed made a noise.
'Eek!' he said.

'I've got
an idea!'

He ran away and when he came back,
he was holding a very large stick of
candy-floss.

'Cudweed!' cried Solstice. 'This is no time to think about eating!'

Very carefully, Cudweed walked towards the elephant.
People screamed.
They thought Cudweed was going to be squashed, but instead, the elephant stopped charging about.

It came over to Cudweed, and began eating the candy-floss.

'Gasp!' said Solstice.

Slowly Cudweed backed into the cage, holding out the candy-floss.

Then he left the elephant in the cage,
while he backed out of the door again.

As soon as he had, someone shut the door.

'Gasp!' said Solstice again. 'Who would have thought that elephants like candy-floss so much?'

Cudweed smiled.
'I did,' he said.

'Cudweed,' said Solstice. 'That is the cleverest thing you have ever done.'

Their parents agreed, and when they heard the story of what Cudweed had done, and how he had saved the town, they decided to give him a big reward.

'Cudweed,' said his father. 'As a reward for this clever thing you have done, you can choose your own birthday present.

From Catchem's pet shop!

Yes.

You can choose anything you like!

Anything!'

Cudweed's mother looked worried.

'Anything, dear? Is that a good idea?'
she asked as she passed Cudweed
another large slice of chocolate
birthday cake.

Cudweed's father whispered back,
so only she could hear.
'It's all right,' he said. 'I phoned the
shop. The most dangerous thing they
have in stock right now is a
grumpy duck.'

Cudweed had already run off to the pet shop, dragging Solstice behind him.

What none of them saw was a van driving past.

On its side it had the words
CATCHEM'S PET SHOP.
And from inside it came a chattering
and whooping noise, the sort of noise
that small monkeys make.

Later, back in the castle, Cudweed
showed his new pet to his mother
and father.

'You did say anything,' said his mother.

'Yes,' said his father unhappily. 'I did.'

They all stood around, looking at a
small but very, very noisy monkey.

'What are you going to call it?'
asked Solstice.

Cudweed thought for a long time.
'Fellah!' he said in the end.

His father groaned.

'Ugh! Cudweed! Go to your room!
And take that monkey with you!'

So Cudweed did.
He ran off to his room, taking Fellah
the monkey with him.

The best birthday present ever.

Did you enjoy the story?
Can you remember the things
that happened?

Why is Cudweed worried about his
birthday?

What does Solstice think Cudweed
would like for his birthday?

What does Cudweed think would be a really good idea to have as a pet? Do his parents agree?

One of Cudweed's birthday presents is a book called *The Pea*. Would you like to read a book called *The Pea*? What's your favourite book?

Would you like to have as a pet...

...an elephant?

...a crocodile?

...a python?

...a tiger?

If you had a pet, what would its name be?

What's your favourite animal?

Why does Cudweed decide to let the elephant out of its cage?

Do you like candy-floss? Do you think elephants like candy-floss?

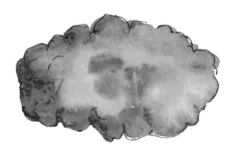

What does Cudweed decide is the best birthday present ever?

Geronimo Stilton

ATTACK of the BANDIT CATS

PUFFIN BOOKS

Published by the Penguin Group
Penguin Books Ltd, 80 Strand, London WC2R 0RL, England
Penguin Group (USA) Inc., 375 Hudson Street, New York, New York 10014, USA
Penguin Group (Canada), 90 Eglinton Avenue East, Suite 700, Toronto, Ontario, Canada M4P 2Y3
(a division of Pearson Penguin Canada Inc.)
Penguin Ireland, 25 St Stephen's Green, Dublin 2, Ireland (a division of Penguin Books Ltd)
Penguin Group (Australia), 707 Collins Street, Melbourne, Victoria 3008, Australia
(a division of Pearson Australia Group Pty Ltd)
Penguin Books India Pvt Ltd, 11 Community Centre, Panchsheel Park, New Delhi – 110 017, India
Penguin Group (NZ), 67 Apollo Drive, Rosedale, Auckland 0632, New Zealand
(a division of Pearson New Zealand Ltd)
Penguin Books (South Africa) (Pty) Ltd, Block D, Rosebank Office Park, 181 Jan Smuts Avenue, Parktown
North, Gauteng 2193, South Africa

Penguin Books Ltd, Registered Offices: 80 Strand, London WC2R 0RL, England

puffinbooks.com

English-language edition first published in Great Britain by Scholastic Children's Books 2004
This edition published in Great Britain in Puffin Books 2013
001

Geronimo Stilton names, characters and related indicia are copyright, trademark and exclusive
license of Atlantyca S.p.A. All Rights Reserved.
The moral right of the author has been asserted

Text by Geronimo Stilton
Original cover by Matt Wolf, revised by Lorenzo Chiavini
Illustrations by Matt Wolf, revised by Flavio Ferron, Andrea Denegri and Silvia Bigolin
Graphics by Merenguita Gingermouse, Angela Simone and Benedetta Galante
Special thanks to Kathryn Cristaldi
Original cover design by Ursula Albano
Interior layout by Madalina Stefan Blanton

Text, illustrations and English translation copyright © 2000, 2004,
Edizioni Piemme S.p.A., Corso Como 15, 20154 Milano – Italy
International Rights copyright © Atlantyca S.p.A., via Leopardi 8, 20123 Milano – Italy

Original title: *Il galeone dei gatti pirati*
Based on an original idea by Elisabetta Dami
www.geronimostilton.com

Stilton is the name of a famous English cheese. It is a registered trademark of the
Stilton Cheesemakers' Association. For more information go to www.stiltoncheese.com

British Library Cataloguing in Publication Data
A CIP catalogue record for this book is available from the British Library

ISBN: 978–0–141–34134–7

www.greenpenguin.co.uk